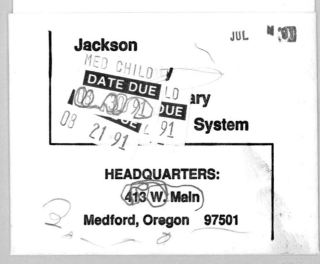

THREE GOOD
BLANKETS

THREE GOOD BLANKETS

by Ida Luttrell

illustrated by

Michael McDermott

Atheneum 1990 New York

To Phyllis and the group
—I. L.

Text copyright © 1990 by Ida Luttrell
Illustrations copyright © 1990 by Michael McDermott

Atheneum
Macmillan Publishing Company
866 Third Avenue, New York, NY 10022
Collier Macmillan Canada, Inc.
First Edition
Printed in Hong Kong
10 9 8 7 6 5 4 3 2 1
Library of Congress Cataloging-in-Publication Data
Luttrell, Ida.
Three good blankets/Ida Luttrell; illustrated by Michael
McDermott.—1st ed.   p.   cm.
Summary: To her grown children's dismay, an old woman shares her
new blankets with her donkey, goat, and dog.
ISBN 0-689-31586-4
[1. Blankets—Fiction. 2. Kindness—Fiction. 3. Animals—
Fiction.] I. McDermott, Michael, ill. II. Title. III. Title: 3
good blankets.
PZ7.L97953Th   1990   89-36353
[E]—dc20 CIP AC

There once was an old woman who lived in a cracky old house up high on a hill. The house had cracks over the windows and cracks under the doors. There were cracks in the walls and cracks in the floors.

When winter came, the wind blew cold across the valley and up the hill and through the cracks, and filled the house with shivers and chills. The old woman huddled close to her poor little fire. She covered herself with the only blanket she had—an old one, tattered and gray and full of holes.

She gazed at the fire and thought of Garibaldi, her faithful donkey, out in his stall with the icy wind whipping about his ears. Her own ears grew cold and she began to tremble. The old woman thought of Willanna, her little milk goat, out in her pen with the raw wind nipping her nose. Her own nose became numb and she began to shake. She saw Herman, her tired old dog, keeping watch by the door with the cruel wind gnawing at his toes, and her own feet felt like two blocks of ice. The old woman turned blue and her teeth began to chatter.

Just then, her daughter, Rilda, came knocking at the door.

"Mama," she said, "you must leave this house. It can't be fixed. For every crack my brothers and I have filled, two more appear. My house is snug. Come and move to the village and live with me. You could sit by the window and watch the people pass by. I have little enough, but what I have I will share with you."

"And what about my donkey, my goat, and my dog?" the old woman asked.

"You won't need them," said Rilda.

"But they need me," said the old woman, and she refused to leave her cracky old house.

The next day, while the old woman gathered sticks for her fire and Garibaldi carried them to the house, Rilda came again. She brought her mother a good blanket, all soft and blue.

"Mama," she said, "if you must stay in your cracky old house, here is something to keep you warm."

"Oh, thank you," the old woman said. "You are a devoted daughter and a kind one, too."

That night, the wind howled and cried and pried its way into the cracky little house. The old woman snuggled deep under the good blanket and thought of Garibaldi. He had no blanket or fire to warm his ears. So she took the good blanket, all soft and blue, and went to his stall.

Garibaldi was so cold he could not sleep. He twitched and stomped and stamped his feet.

"Dear faithful one," the old woman said, "you carry the sticks to build my fire. You should not have to suffer the cold." And she wrapped him in her good, soft blanket, taking special care to cover his ears.

Garibaldi laughed at the wind, closed his eyes, and began to snore.

When Rilda came again, she found the old woman stirring a pot on the fire. The shabby gray blanket was over her shoulders.

"Mama," Rilda said, "where is the good blanket I gave you?"

"A faithful donkey needs a soft blanket," her mother said.

"Cover Garibaldi with your blanket full of holes," said Rilda. "I will go and bring the good blanket back."

"What!" cried the old woman. "And have me smell like a donkey? I would not think of using a blanket that has been on a donkey."

"You are right," said Rilda.

So the daughter went down the hill, through the village, and across a field to her brother Hans's house—a small one for sure, but not so poor as their mother's.

"Hans," Rilda said, "Mama is freezing in that cracky old house up on the hill. Do you have a good blanket she can use?"

"Of course," said Hans. And with a good blanket, all fluffy and white, he started across the field, through the village, and up the hill. He found his mother milking her goat, Willanna. The little goat filled the pail with sweet, rich milk.

"Here, Mama," Hans said, "take this good blanket. It will keep you warm."

"You are a worthy son," his mother said, "and a thoughtful one, too."

That night, when the sun went down and the wind came up, the old woman took the fluffy white blanket and went to bed. But each time she closed her eyes, she saw Willanna, cold in her pen, with nothing to keep the wind off her nose. The old woman took her good blanket and went to Willanna's pen. Willanna was too cold to rest. She ran from one end of the pen to the other, bucking and kicking at the cold winter wind.

"Generous little goat," the old woman said, "you keep milk and cheese on my table. It is only right that you should be warm." And the old woman put the good blanket, all fluffy and white, over Willanna, being careful to cover her nose. Willanna curled up in a corner of the pen and, warm at last, went to sleep.

With cold feet, the old woman crept into her bed and tried to sleep under her old gray blanket full of holes.

The next day was colder than the day before. Hans came to see if his mother was warm enough under her fluffy white blanket.

Instead, he saw his mother, wrapped in the ragged gray blanket, fanning the fire.

"Where is the good blanket I brought you?" Hans asked.

"A generous milk goat needs a warm blanket," said his mother.

"Mama," said Hans, "I will get the good blanket. Willanna can have your old blanket full of holes."

"What!" the old woman cried. "The good blanket has been on a goat with a coat full of burrs. The burrs will scratch me and hurt me and prick my skin. I can't use a blanket that has been on a goat."

"That is true," said Hans.

Straight away, he hurried down the hill, through the village, and past the mill to his brother Jacob's house.

"Jacob," he said, "our poor old mother has only an old gray blanket full of holes to keep herself warm. She gave Rilda's blanket to the donkey and mine to the goat. We have no more blankets. Do you have a good one to spare?"

"Certainly," said Jacob, who had very little, but still more than his poor old mother.

"Good," said Hans. "See that she keeps it for herself. You are the eldest. She will listen to you."

Jacob took a good blanket, all cozy and fresh, and went past the mill, through the village, and up the hill to his mother's house.

"Here is a good blanket," said Jacob. "Put it on your bed and sleep warmly tonight."

"You are a dependable son and a loving one, too," his mother said.

"And, Mama," said Jacob, "Garibaldi has a blanket, Willanna has a blanket, and Herman has a thick coat of his own, so he does not need one."

"That is sensible enough," said his mother. "You were always one to use your head."

With that, Jacob hastened down the hill to tell Rilda and Hans of his success.

When night came, the wind whipped through the cracks in the house like slivers of ice. In his stall, Garibaldi settled down under his good blanket, all soft and blue. In her pen, Willanna rested under her good blanket, all fluffy and white. Bundled in her good blanket, all cozy and fresh, the old woman sat by the fire and tried to warm her feet.

Wolves howled at the foot of the hill. Herman leaped from the doorstep and ran across the frozen ground, against the bitter wind, and chased the wolves away. The old woman waited for him by the door.

"Poor Herman," the old woman said, "you have kept me
safe all these years. Coat or no coat, your feet are still cold.
You deserve a good blanket to keep you well." And she put
the good blanket, all cozy and fresh, over Herman. She was
careful to cover his shivering toes. Herman breathed a
grateful sigh and licked her hand.

The old woman built up her fire, heated some milk, and
prepared for bed. She covered herself with her ragged old
blanket, and soon, feeling quite warm, she fell asleep.

Rilda, Hans, and Jacob came back the next day to see if their mother was warm under her fresh, cozy blanket.

"What is this?" cried Jacob. "You gave the good blanket to the dog! Herman does not smell like a donkey and he has no burrs in his coat. Cover yourself with the good blanket. Give Herman your old blanket full of holes."

"And be bitten by fleas?" said the old woman. "I would never sleep under a blanket that has been on a dog!"

"Fleas are something to think about," said Rilda.

"But we have no more good blankets!" Hans said.

"No matter," said the old woman. "The blankets you gave me serve me well. A goat that sleeps warm gives twice the milk, and a donkey that gets rest carries double the wood. Hot milk warms my inside and a hot fire warms my outside, so the old gray blanket is all that I need."

"But the dog—" said Jacob. "The blanket you gave Herman does not thaw your feet."

"Ah, but it does," said the old woman. "A loyal dog keeping watch is the warmest cover of all."

So her children went home happy, and the old woman
who lived in the cracky old house kept herself warm with
three good blankets and one full of holes.